pilot's launch position

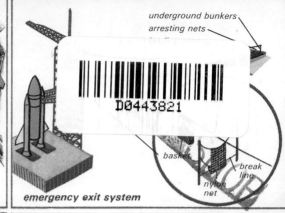

underground bunkers
arresting nets

basket

break line

nylon net

emergency exit system

entering the atmosphere

flight path

tracking on the ground

runway

runway entry point

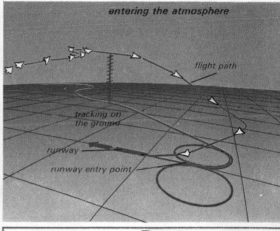

xtravehicular activity

release and deployment

1

2

3

4

5

satellite released

6

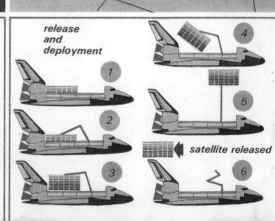

From the moment man first looked up and saw birds flying through the air, he wanted to fly as well. By way of balloons and gliders, airships and autogiros, he found some strange answers to his problem. Here is the story of how man took to the air and all the developments along the way which led to the latest technology involved in space flights and the exploration of the solar system.

Acknowledgments

The author and publishers wish to acknowledge the use of additional illustrative material as follows:

Anglia Television Ltd, page 8; BBC Hulton Picture Library, page 6 (top) and page 15; Austin J Brown, Aviation Picture Library, title page and pages 11 (two), 13 (bottom), 14 (bottom), 20 (bottom), 21 (bottom) copyright Stephen Piercey, 24 (two), 25 (top) copyright Graham Finch, 25 (bottom), 26, 27, 28, 31 (top) copyright Graham Finch, 34, 50 (two), and back cover copyright Graham Finch; Tim Clark, page 44 (top); Daily Telegraph Colour Library, pages 36 (bottom) copyright Space Frontiers Ltd, 37 (two) copyright Space Frontiers Ltd, 40 copyright NASA; Jeremy Flack/Aviation Photographs Ltd, pages 14 (top), 18, 21 (top), 22 (two), 23 (two), 29, 30, 31 (bottom); Hewlett Packard Ltd, page 44 (bottom); Keystone Press Ltd, page 7; Lockheed Company, page 51; Graham Marlow, page 10; R G Moulton, ASP Ltd, pages 4 and 5; NASA, page 35; Roger Pollard, cover; Popperfoto, pages 12, 19 and 36 (top); Rockwell International Inc, page 47; Royal Aircraft Establishment Farnborough (Space and New Concepts Department), page 45; Smithsonian Institution (photo A 38626B), page 13.

British Library Cataloguing in Publication Data

Hoyle, Geoffrey
    Flight.—(Achievements. Series 601; no. 1)
    1. Aeronautics—History—Juvenile literature
    I. Title   II. Series
    629.133′09   TL515
    ISBN 0-7214-0833-8

First edition

© LADYBIRD BOOKS LTD MCMLXXXIV

Flight

by Geoffrey Hoyle
illustrated by Gerald Witcomb MSIAD

Ladybird Books Loughborough

A dream comes true

If thoughts were wings, people would have flown under their own power thousands of years ago. Unassisted flight is one of our oldest dreams.

An ultra light aircraft – Gossamer Albatross

To start with, people tried everything from aerial paddles to cloth or feather-covered wings. The fact that they could have built a glider using things like wood, fabric and rope was overlooked, because they were so sure that the way to fly was to copy the birds. Before they could think of building a glider, however, they had to understand the way air flows round a moving body.

It wasn't until 1977 that people first succeeded in propelling themselves through the air. On 23rd August Bryan Allen, a former racing cyclist, pedalled Dr Paul MacCready's *Gossamer Condor* over a 1.8 kilometres (1.15 miles) course in 6 minutes 22.5 seconds, and found himself in the record books. His plane was built from plastic sheeting, piano wire, aluminium and carbon fibre tubing, and only weighed 32 kg (70 lb). Two years later the same team flew across the English Channel in *Gossamer Albatross.* Pedalling hard, they managed to stay just above the waves, and reached a speed of 19 kmh (12 mph).

Gossamer Albatross crossing the English Channel

Balloons and airships

The first balloon to carry people was made by the Montgolfier brothers. It flew in 1783. Their balloon *(shown left)* was filled with hot air. Soon after, another Frenchman, J A C Charles, made an ascent in a hydrogen-filled balloon. Neither of these balloons could fly very far.

Over two hundred years had to pass before balloons could fly the Atlantic. Since balloons rely on the wind for propulsion, it has always been difficult to control their flight. One answer to this came from yet another Frenchman, Henri Giffard. In 1852, he put a small steam engine into an airship filled with hydrogen, and coaxed it over a distance of 27 kilometres (17 miles) at a speed of 8 kmh (5 mph).

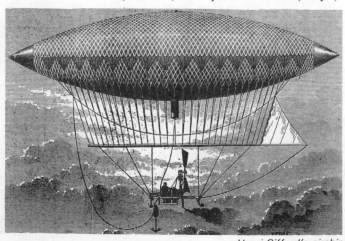

Henri Giffard's airship

6

The Hindenburg

It was to be another fifty years before Count Ferdinand von Zeppelin was able to build the first rigid airship.

But the new airship had many problems, not least the enormous fire risk from the highly inflammable hydrogen used to take them into the air. Major accidents such as the loss of the British *R101* en route for India with many people aboard and the explosion of the *Hindenburg* at Lakehurst, New Jersey, proved their downfall. Today the use of gases like helium has overcome the fire risks aboard airships, but they have never been popular. As the aeroplane developed, airships began to disappear.

Control, thrust and lift

To be able to fly at all, airships must be lighter than air. So how does an aeroplane fly? It is after all *much* heavier than air.

One of the first men to think about controlling a heavier than air vehicle was Sir George Cayley. He built model gliders to test his theories, finally building a glider which carried a man in 1854. His theories gave rise to the science we call *aerodynamics:* that is, the way air flows round a moving body, such as a glider or an aeroplane. Control, thrust and lift are all part of aerodynamics, and are all necessary to fly an aeroplane.

Modern day replica of a glider designed by Sir George Cayley in the first half of the 19th century

Sir George Cayley

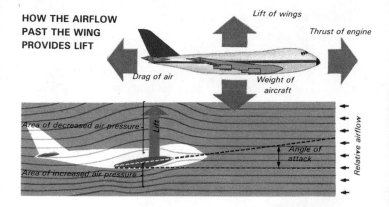

HOW THE AIRFLOW PAST THE WING PROVIDES LIFT

Lift of wings

Thrust of engine

Drag of air

Weight of aircraft

Area of decreased air pressure

Lift

Area of increased air pressure

Angle of attack

Relative airflow

Control This is provided by having surfaces that move independently of the main part of the plane. Ailerons (see page 16) and a rudder will make the plane turn, and elevators will make it dive or climb. As they move, pressure from the airflow increases in certain places, making the plane go in one particular direction.

Thrust A propeller or jet provides thrust to overcome air resistance, and to make the plane move.

Lift For a plane to fly, it must be given a lifting force at least equal to its own weight. It gets this force from its forward speed which the wings convert into what we call *lift*. The wings are of a special curved shape, which gives better lift than a flat shape. They are fixed to the plane at an angle with the front (leading) edge slightly higher than the back (trailing) edge, and this also helps to give better lift.

Although Sir George Cayley was very successful with his aerodynamic theories, he was ahead of his time in his search for a power unit to provide thrust for his gliders. He had to experiment with engines driven by gunpowder or steam.

Gliders and kites

A young German civil engineer Otto Lilienthal began to build on the work done by Sir George Cayley.

His flying experiments were carried out with gliders which he controlled by leaning his body to and fro and from side to side. Hang gliders today fly in much the same way.

Some of Lilienthal's gliders were monoplanes, and others were biplanes. Between 1891 and 1896 he managed to take them as high as 230 m (750 ft).

A Lilienthal glider – late 19th century

He wrote up all his work very carefully and it was published, becoming the standard work on flight. His valuable work in aviation was cut short when he crashed and was killed in 1896.

Next to take up the challenge of manned flight was Octave Chanute of Chicago. He set up a glider camp in 1896-7, and some two thousand flights were made, gathering important information on the problems of control and balance.

A modern hang glider

The glider as we know it today didn't evolve until 1914. The modern glider rises on the *thermals* or updraughts of air, rather than simply just gliding horizontally.

A glider dumping water ballast

The internal combustion engine

The work of Sir George Cayley, Otto Lilienthal, Octave Chanute and others, proved of immense value to Wilbur and Orville Wright when they started to design aeroplanes. There was still the problem of a suitable power unit, however. No aeroplane was ever going to fly without one.

The invention of the internal combustion engine and the discovery of the fuel that makes it work provided the answer for almost all the first half of the twentieth century. The engines built for the car industry however were just too heavy. The Nikolaus August Otto gas engine of 1880 weighed 199 kg (440 lb) for every horsepower it produced. That was fifty times too heavy for use in an aeroplane. By 1900 Gottlieb Daimler had made great improvements in engine design for cars, bringing the power-to-weight ratio nearer to 5 kg (9 lb) for every horsepower.

But when the Wright brothers began to build *Flier 1*

The first successful powered flight by the Wright brothers in 1903 – the Wright Flier

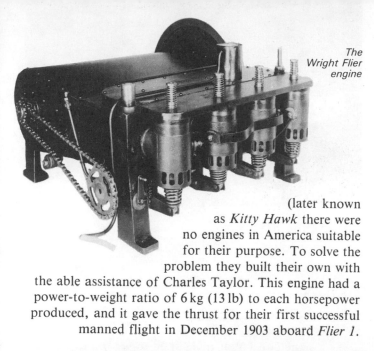

(later known
as *Kitty Hawk* there were
no engines in America suitable
for their purpose. To solve the
problem they built their own with
the able assistance of Charles Taylor. This engine had a
power-to-weight ratio of 6 kg (13 lb) to each horsepower
produced, and it gave the thrust for their first successful
manned flight in December 1903 aboard *Flier 1*.

Rolls Royce Olympus engine as used in Concorde

13

A Vickers Gunbus – World War I

Power from the piston

Wilbur and Orville Wright and those who followed, like Louis Bleriot, proved that manned flight was possible. The planes they flew were however only lightweight structures, made from wood and canvas. If air transport was to become important, more engine power was going to be needed.

It took the Great War of 1914-18 to get things moving. Up to then, aircraft were flimsy and kite-like, with unreliable engines. They couldn't fly very high, or very fast, or very far. At their best, they could climb to 1000 m (3000 ft) and fly at 113 kmh (70 mph) for perhaps 323 kilometres (200 miles). At worst, these engines could barely give enough speed for the aircraft to leave the

A Fokker Triplane – World War I

ground! New lightweight engines had to be developed. Soon aircraft were being produced that could climb to 4572 m (15000 ft), fly at speeds of more than 160 kmh (100 mph) and carry more people and more weapons.

14

At the end of the Great War, bombers and fighters, no longer needed as such, became passenger and freight (airmail) aeroplanes, or stunt aircraft. Many factories making aeroplanes had to close because of the lack of demand for new aircraft. It wasn't until the late 1920s that the aircraft industry began to prosper once more.

Public interest in flying was kept alive during this period by the exploits of the record breakers and other daring aviation feats. In 1922 the World Air Speed record stood at 359 kmh (222.96 mph). In 1927, it was raised to 519 kmh (322.60 mph). People flew their machines further and further, and higher and higher.

Captain John Alcock and Lieutenant Arthur Brown flew across the Atlantic in 1919, then in 1930 Charles Kingsford Smith flew round the world. In the same year as the Atlantic crossing – 1919 – Roland Rohlfs flew to a height of 10610 m (34910 ft). Eleven years later Lieutenant Apollo Soucek bettered this with a height of 13120 m (43166 ft). By the 1930s engines were much more powerful and looked very different from that built by the Wright Brothers.

Alcock and Brown

The shape

While the aero engine was becoming more and more efficient, the shape of the aeroplane was also changing rapidly.

The Wright biplane was soon seen to be only one of several shapes that could fly. By 1909 the forms that the aeroplane was going to take over the next thirty years were emerging. The monoplane arrived in the shape of the *Bleriot XI* and the *Levavasseur Antoinette*. Both had the engine in the nose, a long body or *fuselage,* and a tail unit. The most important developments during this period took place in France where for example Henri Farman introduced *ailerons,* giving the pilot side to side control. Although the biplane was in general easier to fly, it didn't have the speed or rate of climb of the single wing design. By 1915 the German designer Hugo Junkers had produced monoplanes with *cantilever* wings that were self-supporting and needed no bracing. These machines, made entirely from metal, were the pace setters of the decade.

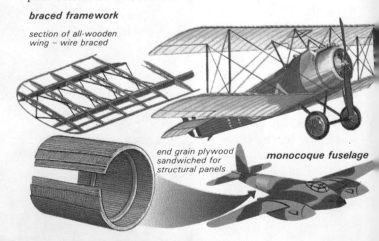

braced framework

section of all-wooden wing – wire braced

end grain plywood sandwiched for structural panels

monocoque fuselage

Lockheed Vega

The 1920s brought one other important new idea. The covering or skin of the aircraft – in wood and later in metal – now carried the load, instead of having a braced wood or metal framework covered with a light fabric. This idea – called the monocoque or single shell fuselage – also proved to suit the retractable undercarriage which appeared in 1920 on the American *Dayton-Wright RB* racer. As speeds increased, fixed undercarriages produced so much wind resistance that extra engine power was needed to overcome it. As soon as the landing wheels were retracted, the plane became smoother and faster.

Towards the end of the 1920s the idea of the streamlined monocoque fuselage was quickly accepted in America. By 1927 planes like the *Lockheed Vega* began to appear using 'stressed skin' ideas. The beauty of this design was that there were no bracing struts inside the aeroplane. This meant that a fuselage could have over a third less cross-section than other designs while still carrying the same weight. This saved on materials, and reduced both weight and wind resistance so that less engine power and fuel were needed to drive the plane.

The aeroplane was ready for its next leap forward – into load-carrying for both civilian and military uses.

The beginning of vertical lift machines

Perhaps the ideal form of aeroplane is one that takes off and lands vertically, so that an elaborate airfield isn't needed. The principles that make such vehicles as the helicopter and autogiro fly were known to the toy makers of China many thousands of years ago. So that they can hover as well as take off and land vertically, lift must be developed by driving the rotors through the air. Launoy and Bienvenu used this principle in 1784 to demonstrate how a model helicopter flies.

Chinese flying toy

This demonstration gave Sir George Cayley the idea of making his own models. He soon realised however that to make a helicopter fly, enormous amounts of engine power would be required. Steam engines were tried, but with little success.

The Wright brothers thought about building helicopters but decided that it would be easier to make an aeroplane – which is still true even today!

In the early days a Frenchman, Paul Cornu, made the first helicopter flights in 1907. None however lasted more than a few seconds.

·It was the 1920s before any real success came to Vertical Take Off and Landing aircraft, known as VTOL. Spaniard Juan de la Cierva's autogiros could

Cierva autogiro

G-ACUU

sustain flight, and in 1928 he flew one from London to Paris. Up to Cierva's death in 1936, his machines were popular, but interest then waned in favour of the helicopter. By the mid 1930s engines were producing the right kind of power-to-weight ratio, and in 1936 Heinrich Focke built the first practical helicopter. As his ideas developed, machines were soon flying at over 113 kmh (70 mph) at heights up to 3334 m (11000 ft), and in 1940 he built the first passenger-carrying helicopter. Focke's design used two rotors rotating in opposite directions, set on outriggers. This was to start the German and Russian tradition of multiple counter-rotators.

Igor Sikorsky flying one of his first practical helicopters

It was a Russian engineer, Igor Sikorsky, who emigrated to America in 1917, who established the single main rotor and small tail rotor of modern helicopter design. Up till then, the machine's tendency to twist in the opposite direction from the rotation of the rotor blades (called *torque*) was a great problem in helicopter design. The tail rotor solved this.

The start of commercial aviation

Carrying fare-paying passengers by air really began in 1910 with Count von Zeppelin's airship service, *Delag*. But it was the end of the First World War before international air transportation services using aeroplanes sprang

Inside an early commercial aircraft

up throughout Europe. All kinds of planes, from converted single or twin seater fighter planes, to modified *Handley Page* and *Farman* bombers, were in use. The seating arrangements were crude at best – usually just a row of wicker chairs. In flight the aircraft were noisy, cold and unpressurised.

By 1920 European governments were encouraging the formation of national airlines like Imperial Airways Ltd (now British Airways) and Aeropostale (now Air France). By the late 1920s passengers were regularly carried nationwide within the USA.

Then people began to find themselves travelling in reliable, comfortable, pressurised purpose-built passenger planes. The *Douglas DC1* for example and its most famous child the *DC3 Dakota* (below), forerunner of today's jet shapes, came into being.

Along with the great improvements in aircraft design came the need for better navigation and communications systems. Landing in fog for example – called 'blind landing' – had to be made safer.

An early instrument panel

As a result of research, the first completely 'blind' flight in a plane with a fully hooded cockpit, piloted by James H Doolittle, took place in 1929. The pilot couldn't see where he was going, and had to rely on instruments alone.

With all these developments, travelling by air became both safer and more comfortable. Commercial aviation had begun to establish itself.

In the cockpit of a Boeing 757

The jet engine

If the developments of the first thirty years of
aviation in the twentieth century were outstanding, then
the quiet research of Frank Whittle was revolutionary.
In 1928 he published his work on the use of gas turbines
for aircraft. Two years later he registered his design
for the jet engine at the Patent Office. In Germany
Hans von Ohain was also working on the same subject,
taking out his patents in 1935.

It was the summer of 1939 when the first jet-powered
aircraft flew. It was a German one – a *Heinkel He 178*
flew from Rostock in Germany. The first British test
flight came almost two years later when a *Gloster E28/39*
equipped with the first Whittle engine flew from
Cranwell, Lincolnshire. Not long after, a *Bell W-IX*
aircraft with a Whittle engine flew in America.

From then on, jet fighters developed rapidly. By 1944
the Germans were flying the *Messerschmitt Me 262*

*Messerschmitt
Me 262 (above)*

*Engine of
Me 262*

while in Britain the slower
Gloster F9/40 Meteor was in
production but not yet in use.
At the same time, in America,
the *Lockheed XP-80* was also
undergoing test flights.

*Gloster Meteor
(above) and instrument
panel (below)*

Although the Germans
seemed to be ahead, it was
Whittle's, not Ohain's, engine
design that became the father
of the post-war jet. The reason
for this lay in the war time exchange
of technology between the Allied Powers.
The Whittle engine was sent to both
the USA and
USSR.

*Sir Frank Whittle with
one of his early engines*

23

Comet airliner

The jet engine in civil aircraft

The coming of jet power changed every aspect of aviation. Not many years after the first jet-powered flight, speeds of over 1216 kmh (760 mph) (the speed of sound) and more were within reach.

The first jet-powered aeroplane to appear on the commercial routes was the British *De Havilland Comet* which began service in 1952. Unfortunately the *Comet* had two serious accidents caused by metal fatigue and the plane was grounded. When it was withdrawn from service, the American Boeing Company worked round the clock to perfect their airliner, the *Boeing 707*. In 1958 the *707* went into service, along with the return of the *Comet*.

Boeing 747 (jumbo jet)

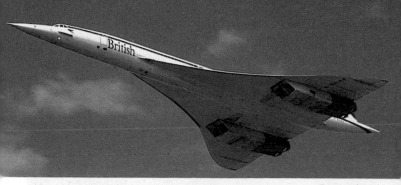

Concorde

From this point on, a bevy of airliners were produced. By 1971 few propeller-driven planes were left in commercial service. The 1970s also saw the structural change to wide-bodied jets like the *Boeing 747,* which could carry more than four hundred people at over 1000 kmh (625 mph). With the rise in world oil prices since 1973, research on quieter, cost saving airliners began. It has produced yet another generation of commercial aircraft like the *Airbus A310* and the *BAe 146* and *147.*

At the same time as the steady improvement in subsonic airliners was taking place, supersonic airliners were born, starting with the Anglo/French *Concorde* which went into service in 1976, and the Soviet *Tupolev TU 144* (now withdrawn from service). These could fly at twice the speed of sound.

Tupolev TU 144

Tornado

Military aircraft in the jet age

The almost unlimited power of the jet engine also revolutionised military aircraft.

By the 1960s most military and naval combat aircraft were jet-powered and could fly at speeds greater than the speed of sound. Some experimental aircraft like the *Bell X* series were even capable of twice the speed of sound and more, using rocket power.

As aircraft speeds jumped to Mach 2, 3 (*ie*, twice and three times the speed of sound) and beyond, a new problem raised its head. How would these speeds affect the human pilot? The inside of a modern fighter looks as though it caters more for the fuel, ammunition, guns, computers, engines and other vital equipment than for the pilot. To some degree this is true, because computers help to fly many of today's military aircraft.

The pilot's cockpit, although cramped, is heated and pressurised for flying at high altitude. He also has to wear pressurised clothing. So that he won't faint from the immense acceleration during high speed manoeuvres, he has to fly almost lying down in his seat. That seat is an *ejector* seat – it has rocket motors that will shoot it from the plane in emergency, and a parachute.

The shape of the fighter plane of today looks very like that of a rocket. The fuselage is usually long, narrow and pointed, with the cockpit set well forward in the nose. Wings are short and usually swept back.

Bombers are smaller than they used to be and can fly at speeds close to those of fighter planes. The jet engine made this possible, producing enormous power for its weight.

Military forces have to be moved quickly to trouble spots, and this requires specialised planes and helicopters. Typical of these transport aircraft is the *Lockheed C-5 Galaxy* which can carry 120 tonnes (118 tons) over 8850 km (5500 miles) at 644 kmh (400 mph).

For short distances, helicopters are used to carry both machines and people. Amongst those developed for these purposes are the *CH 47D Chinook,* the Soviet *M 126 Halo,* the *Puma* and the *Sikorsky CH 54A.*

Jaguar GR 1

STOL and VTOL aircraft

The birth of the jet engine opened up completely new possibilities in aircraft design. Outstanding amongst these ideas were the STOL (short take off and landing) and VTOL (vertical take off and landing) types of aircraft.

Helicopter principles for take off and landing have been used for a number of different designs. There are *convertiplanes*, which have stubby wings as well as a rotor. The wings help with lift at forward speeds, so reducing the load on the rotor. They also help to cut down on the high speed vibration and drag created by the rotor. The convertiplanes do however have one disadvantage compared with ordinary helicopters. They can't hover quite so well, because the rotor pushes a heavy extra load of air down on the wings when hovering.

To avoid this difficulty, several alternatives have been tried. These range from tilting the entire aircraft through 90° after vertical take off from a tail-sitting position, to tilting the engines or the engines and wings in combination. The Rotor Tilt of the *Bell XV 15* is an example.

Bell XV 15

Harrier Jump Jet

Another way is to mount jet engines in the usual horizontal manner and deflect the jetblast downwards with movable vanes to give vertical thrust for take off. As soon as the plane has reached flying height, the vanes are retracted and the aircraft flies on the level. The British *Hawker-Siddeley Harrier Jump Jet* is the most spectacular example of this. It can rise vertically from an area little greater than its own size, then achieve supersonic speed in level flight. It lands by reversing the process.

All direct lift aircraft have certain problems in common. The first is the effect of the slipstream striking the ground. Loose material thrown about is a danger both to the people aboard the aircraft and those on the ground. Next, the whole operation relies on the engines while hovering and while flying at a low speed, just as with a helicopter. Power failure in these circumstances would be a catastrophe.

Entirely different control techniques are required for flying at slow speed, because there is little or no airflow over the aerodynamic surfaces of the plane.

CH 54 Skycrane carrying a bridge section

Helicopters

Although the helicopter is expensive to build and operate, it has become an everyday part of aviation. Its first life-saving mission was in 1944, when an experimental 180 horsepower machine brought blood through a blizzard to victims of a shipboard explosion off the north eastern coast of America. From that point on, it has been used for many different purposes.

In major disasters helicopters are invaluable, whether going to the rescue of those in peril or delivering food and medicine to relief areas.

Few are privately owned because of the high cost of buying and maintaining one. Yet the use of helicopters in business and commercial applications grows daily. Because they are easily manoeuvred and can hover, they are the ideal answer for such activities as prospecting, checking remote power lines, finding shipping routes through ice fields, crop spraying, insect control and conservation operations. Municipal and highway authorities, police and fire departments, ambulances, photographers, and news agencies all find more and more uses for the smaller machines with two to four seats.

Larger helicopters handle many unusual assignments. They lift and move timber, minerals, television masts and construction equipment.

Chinook carrying a tank

Helicopter fights a fire

Oil companies operating wells far out in coastal waters use fleets of helicopters. Cross-country pipe lines can be checked and power companies' cables, heavy machinery – even poles and steel towers – are ferried by helicopters to sites that cannot be reached by road.

The larger twin-rotor helicopters are now used for such jobs as shuttling passengers between airports and city centres.

31

Birth of the rocket

Rocket power has been used for hundreds of years —
for signalling, for firework displays, and for military
purposes. Nearly a hundred years ago scientists saw that
rocket power was the key to exploring space. In the run
up to man's first flight in space four men played an
important part.

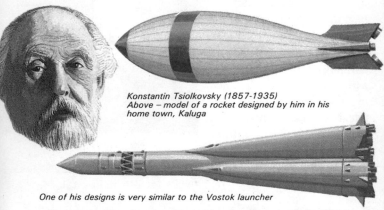

Konstantin Tsiolkovsky (1857-1935)
Above – model of a rocket designed by him in his
home town, Kaluga

One of his designs is very similar to the Vostok launcher

A young Russian mathematics teacher was the first
man to understand the importance of rocket power and
why the use of powder propellants in rockets was
limited. He was Konstantin Eduardovich Tsiolkovsky
who published his first article on space travel in 1895.
He saw that if liquid propellants such as hydrogen and
oxygen rather than powder propellants were used, rocket
engines would be much more efficient. Later he worked
on the theory of space vehicle design, including the idea
of using plant life to produce the oxygen needed so that
humans can breathe on long journeys in space.

In the 1920s and 30s, a man called Robert Hutchings
Goddard built rocket engines. His work helped to

increase the knowledge needed to explore space.

In 1923 another mathematics teacher – Romanian this time – had ideas for huge space vehicles using clusters of motors. Hermann Oberth's theories on electric and 'ion' rocket propulsion were far ahead of his time.

The fourth man, Wernher von Braun, was technical director at the German Army rocket research establishment at Peenemunde, where many technical firsts in rocketry were achieved. Greatest of all was Braun's own brainchild, the A4 long range rocket which reached a speed of 5179 kmh (3200 mph) and covered a distance of nearly 193 km (120 miles). The A4 was renamed the V2, and was soon put into production.

Since that revolutionary breakthrough in rocketry by von Braun a fantastic arsenal of missiles has been produced. There are small anti-tank rockets with a range of 1.6 km (1 mile) and there are monsters that can cover a distance of 9650 km (6000 miles) and more.

The V2 and its successors provided the groundwork for the rockets used in space exploration.

The German, von Braun, and his team were responsible for inventing the V2 rocket and its successors

Computers take over – in the cockpit of a Saab-Fairchild 340

Computers

Modern aircraft and space vehicles are so fast and so complicated that the human pilot has to have reliable help. This has come in the form of the computer which is now a necessary part of every aircraft and space vehicle.

The first production plane using electronics is the *General Dynamics F-16.* Signals given by the pilot through the control stick are transmitted to a computer which then directs the plane. During flight the computer keeps the forward edge of the wing at the best angle for the most efficient use of lift, amongst other details.

Two types of robot navigators are installed in spacecraft (which are mainly controlled in flight by computers). One is a *celestial navigator* which calculates the position from the stars. The second is an *inertial navigator,* which receives its instructions from a gyroscope. Any change of direction or velocity is sensed by the gyroscope in order to change the spaceship's path.

The computer has also made possible a spacecraft's re-entry through the Earth's atmosphere. Without it people might still be bogged down in mathematical calculations, trying to find the very elusive corridor in the Earth's atmosphere through which a space vehicle must return. The path must be plotted exactly so that the space vehicle will not burn up because of friction as it re-enters the atmosphere (see front endpaper).

Computers have also played an important part in the development of the flight simulator, a necessary part of a pilot's training.

The simulator can be programmed to perform an endless number of flight plans and emergencies. It can simulate the pilot's seat of a *Harrier Jump Jet* or an *F-16,* or leisurely cruising the skies in a *Boeing 757,* or a shuttle landing. It is so realistic that sometimes the pilot finds it hard to believe he is not actually flying!

Computers and personnel monitoring every stage of the countdown of Apollo 14's launch

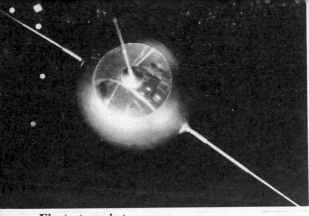

Sputnik 1 – the first artificial Earth satellite

First steps into space

The 'race for space' between the USA and the USSR started in 1957. Towards the end of that year the Russians launched *Sputnik 1,* the first artificial satellite, followed a month later by *Sputnik 2* which carried a dog called 'Liaka'. And the space age began.

The late 1950s saw the launching of a number of unmanned spacecraft of different kinds. Then when John F Kennedy became President in 1961, the American space programme got a terrific boost. A vast space programme was projected, in an effort to surpass the Russian supremacy. In 1961 however the Russians launched their first manned spacecraft, *Vostok 1,* with Yury A Gagarin aboard.

The Russians had produced a launching vehicle which could carry nearly three times as much as the American ones. Both Russian and American space programmes were planning lunar launches, space laboratories and

Telstar launched in 1962 relayed the first TV signals across the Atlantic Ocean

planetary probes. The American Gemini and Russian Voskhod programmes in the mid 1960s showed that people could still function while weightless in space. The Gemini programme was to develop rendezvous and docking techniques in space in preparation

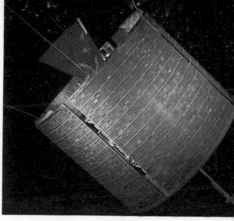

Early Bird satellite

for the Apollo missions. This was immensely important – only a second's delay in launch time would take the target vehicle 8 km (5 miles) beyond the rendezvous point.

The Russian Soyuz programme also looked at complex docking procedures and scientific work, as well as endurance tests for their astronauts. Unfortunately the programme hasn't been completely trouble free. Although they achieved firsts in the longest space flight, there have been accidents and loss of life, just as there have been with the American space programmes.

A satellite being launched from the space shuttle

Spaceships

Enormous power is needed to take a manned space vehicle out from Earth's gravitational field. In rockets like those in a Saturn 5, the necessary power is generated in three stages, the first having the most powerful thrust.

The source of this power can come either from solid or from liquid fuel. Liquid fuel is preferred because it means that the engine can be turned on and off during flight. A solid fuel rocket once alight cannot.

People sometimes think that a rocket is propelled by the gas from its exhausts pushing against the air, but this is not the case. The thrust a rocket engine gives comes from the scientific law which states that for every action there is an equal or opposite reaction. With a rocket engine the gas escapes through the exhausts and as it does so it exerts an equal force in the opposite direction. Watch the way a blown-up balloon flies across the room when the air is suddenly released from it — it is obeying that same law.

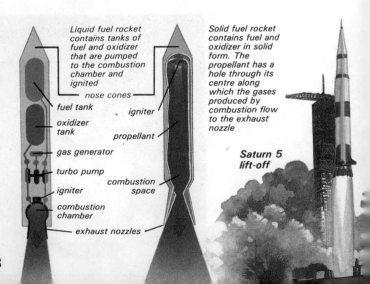

Liquid fuel rocket contains tanks of fuel and oxidizer that are pumped to the combustion chamber and ignited

nose cones

fuel tank

oxidizer tank

gas generator

turbo pump

igniter

combustion chamber

exhaust nozzles

igniter

propellant

combustion space

Solid fuel rocket contains fuel and oxidizer in solid form. The propellant has a hole through its centre along which the gases produced by combustion flow to the exhaust nozzle

Saturn 5 lift-off

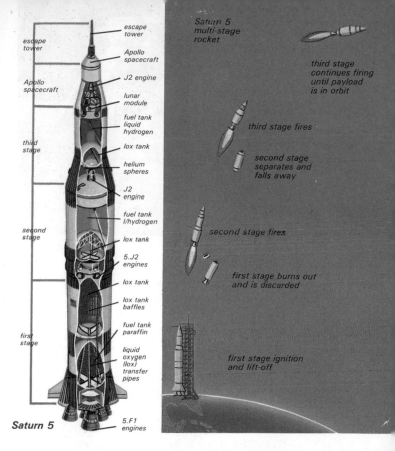

Saturn 5 multi-stage rocket

third stage continues firing until payload is in orbit

third stage fires

second stage separates and falls away

second stage fires

first stage burns out and is discarded

first stage ignition and lift-off

Saturn 5

escape tower

escape tower

Apollo spacecraft

Apollo spacecraft

J2 engine

lunar module

fuel tank liquid hydrogen

third stage

lox tank

helium spheres

J2 engine

fuel tank l/hydrogen

second stage

lox tank

5.J2 engines

lox tank

lox tank baffles

fuel tank paraffin

first stage

liquid oxygen (lox) transfer pipes

5.F1 engines

Spacecraft have to be both light and reliable. Launch vehicles have approximately six million component parts. Every single one must do its job without trouble in difficult circumstances such as extreme variations of temperature and radiation.

The technical challenges presented by the space programmes have brought new technologies, new materials, and powerful new tools of research and production into being.

Moon landing

The Apollo programme

When the Apollo programme was started in 1961 by the National Aeronautics and Space Administration (NASA), it opened the door to one of man's most daring adventures – to put a man on the moon.

Several ideas were considered, but at last a single stage Saturn 5 launch vehicle sent a three-man Apollo spacecraft to the moon. When the spacecraft approached the moon, its own propulsion system put it in orbit. Then the Lunar Module, with two men aboard, separated from the mothership and flew towards the moon's surface. The third man continued to circle the moon in the main part of the spacecraft, called the Command Module.

On 20th June 1969 Neil A Armstrong and Edwin E Aldrin Jr became the first men to walk on the moon. They made scientific observations and collected geological samples, then launched the Lunar Module to rendezvous with the third astronaut, Michael Collins, in the Command Module. Finally, the spacecraft escaped its Lunar Orbit and returned to Earth in triumph.

ignition and lift-off

first stage jettison

second stage ignition

launch escape tower
jettison

second stage jettison

third stage ignition

engine ignition
translunar injection

command and service
modules separate

CSM turnabout

CSM docking with LM

CSM and LM separation
third stage jettison

midcourse turnabout

midcourse correction

lunar orbit insertion

crew transfer to LM

CSM and LM separation

LM descent engine ignition

touchdown

CSM continues in orbit

Route to the moon

Return Route
to Earth

CSM   Command
       Service Module

LM   Lunar Module

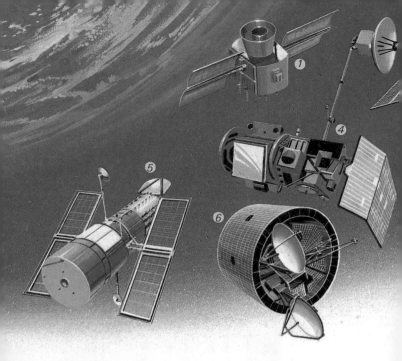

Satellites

Once man had made his first venture into space, new possibilities opened up in many directions.

Research has been carried out by satellites into problems as diverse as cosmic radiation and the causes of space sickness. Many unmanned craft have been used to carry out these experiments. *Pioneer 10,* launched in March 1972, is still going strong. It has already visited Jupiter and Saturn on its journey, and is now flying away from our solar system.

Military satellites are used in communications and to gather information. They can also be used as platforms for launching weapons. This means that they are now a vital part of military technology.

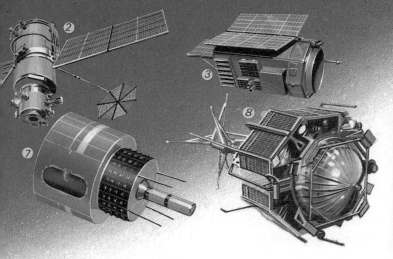

1 military satellite; 2 Russian meteor satellite;
3 Head-A X-ray Astrom satellite; 4 Land-sat;
5 space telescope; 6 navigation satellite;
7 Meteosat – Europe's main weather satellite;
8 Intercosmos 10

The communication satellites are of more practical use. It is now possible to receive and transmit information in pictures and sound for both business and entertainment purposes. New techniques in picture enhancement are so good that a car being driven along a road, for example, can be totally identified when photographed from more than 160 kilometres (100 miles) above the Earth.

Because of satellites, the weather can now be forecast more reliably. Earth survey satellites can also be used to identify water resources, places where the soil is fertile, and the spread of insect pests, amongst other possibilities.

A special class of Earth Orbiting satellite now helps air or sea navigators to fix their positions very accurately, independently of weather conditions.

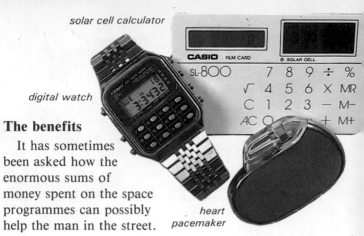

solar cell calculator

digital watch

heart pacemaker

The benefits

It has sometimes been asked how the enormous sums of money spent on the space programmes can possibly help the man in the street.

The answer is – in many ways. To start with, the Americans have a list of twenty thousand items·which have been improved because of space programme research. Those items include heart pacemakers, international phone links, digital watches, high strength glues, and calculators.

Then, in the course of the Apollo programme for example, over half a million people were employed and new management techniques had to be learned. Those techniques are now being applied elsewhere, so that industrial management in general has improved.

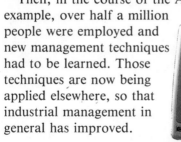

home computer

Looking at Earth from space – a satellite photograph showing the sand dunes of an African desert, and rocks to the north

Weight and power are both important in space flight. For this reason money has been poured into various kinds of miniaturisation such as smaller and smaller computers, and into power sources such as solar-powered panels and long-life batteries.

Space flight has become a testing ground for technologies such as electronics, data processing, machine tools, automation, medical instrumentation and much more. And space itself provides unusual conditions for both medical and industrial research, because of its combination of vacuum and weightlessness. Special photographic techniques also provide back-up information on Earth's resources.

The space shuttle

The Apollo programme with its spectacular moon landings was very expensive. So the next problem was to find a vehicle which could do the same sort of job but could be used more than once.

The answer was the space shuttle, intended to take satellites, military equipment and people to and from space: a 'cargo ship' of space.

The shuttle is the largest and most complicated vehicle to be launched into space. It has five computers on board coping with 325000 operations a second! The use of so many computers on board means that far fewer people are needed on the ground than were needed on previous space missions.

There are three parts to the shuttle: an orbiter; an external fuel tank which holds something like three million litres (over half a million gallons) of liquid oxygen and liquid hydrogen; and two solid fuel rocket boosters.

The orbiter (the 'shuttle') is the heart of the system. It has working and living quarters for as many as seven people, plus a cargo bay large enough to carry the equivalent of five elephants into space.

The problem of getting the great weight of liquid fuel, launch vehicle and shuttle off the ground is solved by using the thrust from the two rocket boosters, which burn aluminium powder. The amount of power provided by these rockets is enough to get 25 jumbo jets airborne!

Once the shuttle is airborne, the three main engines take over and carry the shuttle up to its orbit. Then the external fuel tank is jettisoned and two secondary engines, fed from an internal tank, manoeuvre the shuttle into orbit.

Launching the space shuttle

Bringing the shuttle back so that it can be used again presented another great problem. Every time it descends through the atmosphere, friction heats up the outside body shell to temperatures of over 2500°F. So that the craft won't burn away, it is covered nearly all over with about 34000 heat resistant silicon tiles.

So the difficulties have been overcome and a 'cargo ship' of space now exists. Broken satellites can be retrieved, and laboratory and construction equipment can be both taken into orbit and brought back to Earth.

With the use of the shuttle, space exploration has entered yet another new and exciting stage.

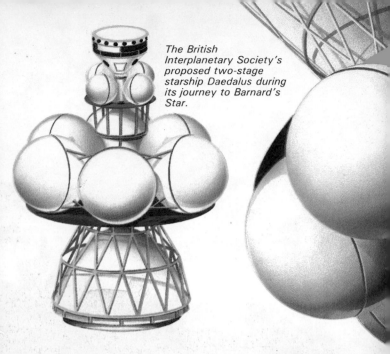

The British Interplanetary Society's proposed two-stage starship Daedalus during its journey to Barnard's Star.

Competition between man and man, company and company, and country and country has always led to new records and new ideas. Because of the competition between Russia and America, the Americans are developing space ideas from the commercial as well as the technological point of view.

Their newest space programmes include the building of a permanent space station. This venture is based on the use of the space shuttle as the main launch vehicle.

The components of the space station will be carried into orbit by the shuttle and will then be assembled. Once it is built, it will provide a base from which a whole host of scientific and industrial studies can take place. One of these days man's dream of passenger services through space may at last be realised!

The proposed Dupont Kevlar lightweight aircraft

Tomorrow

The aircraft of today look very different from those that first flew, at the beginning of the twentieth century. They also fly further and faster, carry more, and are safer in many ways.

Computers now take on some of the load of running and flying an aircraft. Full automation is just around the corner, when all the pilot will have to do is to tell the plane in which direction he wants to fly, at what speed,

A model of the proposed Dornier ND 102

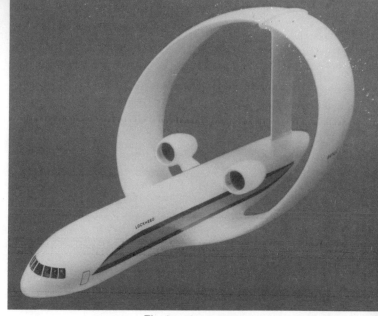

The Lockheed Ring-wing concept model

and it will do the rest. There are so many advances in electronics, satellites and computerisation that navigation is becoming more and more efficient.

The cost of fuel has risen so steeply that all sorts of ideas to lower running costs are being tried. Designers are looking for a wing design with less friction, for example. Then, super glues are taking the place of rivets to join materials together. This leads to lighter aircraft which can carry more, as well as being stronger in themselves.

So changes are going on in every direction. We might well in the future have jet airliners with wings that can pivot 60°, flying at the speed of sound but using much less fuel than present-day airliners.

Who knows what aircraft will look like, even twenty years from now?

INDEX